Happily ever Emma

OTHER BOOKS ABOUT EMMA

℀ ℀ ℀

Only Emma

Not-So-Weird Emma

Super Emma

Best Friend Emma

Excellent Emma

Happily ever Emma

saLLy WaRNeR

Illustrated by

Jamie HaRPeR

Viking

An Imprint of Penguin Group (USA) Inc.

J
War
c2

Viking
Published by Penguin Group
Penguin Young Readers Group, 345 Hudson Street, New York, New York 10014, U.S.A.
Penguin Group (Canada), 90 Eglinton Avenue East, Suite 700, Toronto,
Ontario, Canada M4P 2Y3 (a division of Pearson Penguin Canada Inc.)
Penguin Books Ltd, 80 Strand, London WC2R 0RL, England
Penguin Ireland, 25 St Stephen's Green, Dublin 2, Ireland (a division of Penguin Books Ltd)
Penguin Group (Australia), 250 Camberwell Road, Camberwell, Victoria 3124, Australia
(a division of Pearson Australia Group Pty Ltd)
Penguin Books India Pvt Ltd, 11 Community Centre, Panchsheel Park,
New Delhi – 110 017, India
Penguin Group (NZ), 67 Apollo Drive, Rosedale, North Shore 0632,
New Zealand (a division of Pearson New Zealand Ltd)
Penguin Books (South Africa) (Pty) Ltd, 24 Sturdee Avenue, Rosebank,
Johannesburg 2196, South Africa

Penguin Books Ltd, Registered Offices: 80 Strand, London WC2R 0RL, England

First published in 2010 by Viking, a division of Penguin Young Readers Group

1   3   5   7   9   10   8   6   4   2

LIBRARY OF CONGRESS CATALOGING-IN-PUBLICATION DATA
Warner, Sally.
Happily ever Emma / by Sally Warner ; [art by Jamie Harper].
p. cm.
Summary: Eight-year-old Emma is upset to learn that her mother is dating,
but not passing along a message about a cancelled date makes Emma feels worse.
ISBN 978-0-670-01084-4 (hardcover)
[1. Mothers and daughters—Fiction. 2. Dating (Social customs)—Fiction.
3. Single-parent families—Fiction. 4. Schools—Fiction.] I. Harper, Jamie, ill. II. Title.
PZ7.W24644Hap 2010
[Fic]—dc22
2009049436

Manufactured in China

for Jane, Signe, Cathy, and Penny,
from way back when—S.W.

X X X

For Heather—J.H.

Contents

χ χ χ

Happily ever Emma

✕ 1 ✕

extremely Horrible News!

No matter how bad your school week was, there is always Friday night to look forward to. School can't follow you home, no matter how hard it tries.

I am a person who really likes Friday night, because my mom and I usually go out for dinner then—or to the library and out for an ice cream cone, if Mom has run out of money for the week. Once we skipped the ice cream, and we *still* had fun.

Which is why I cannot believe what my mom just said.

Telescope-eyed goldfish have protruding eyes, but they can't see very well!

"Huh?" I say, goggling at her like a telescope-eyed goldfish.

I want to be a nature scientist when I grow up, and so I try to be as exact as possible when I talk about nature-y things.

Mom blushes a little, which she hardly ever does. "I said that I was going to drop you off at the Scarpettos' house tonight, Emma. For supper and a DVD."

The Scarpettos! "Supper and a DVD with *Anthony*?" I say, trying not to squawk. "But I wanted to go Christmas shopping tonight! And he's only four years old, Mom. What are we going to eat, anyway, weenies and frozen French fries? And what DVD are we going to watch, that cartoon about robots again?"

See, I know Anthony Scarpetto. And I actually like him—as much as an eight-year-old girl can like a four-year-old boy who isn't a relative. Anthony stayed at our house once for a few days, and I even got to babysit him after that, which is how I know about the robot DVD. We watched it *twice*.

Of course, Anthony's mom was at home when I babysat him at his house, since I am still basically a kid. She was cleaning out the garage. But it counts as a real babysitting job, because I got paid.

I'm saving up to buy a nuclear microscope. They cost millions of dollars, but you have to start someplace.

"I don't know what Norah has planned for your supper," Mom says, sounding a little annoyed. "Probably spaghetti, knowing Anthony."

"But Mom," I say, "it's Friday! Friday night is *our* night, yours and mine. And you didn't even warn me." My mouth was watering for Chinese food. Slippery shrimp. And now this! "This is extremely horrible news," I tell her.

"I'm sorry, sweetie," Mom says. She finally looks guilty, and she also looks . . .

I stare at her, and she blushes some more.

"You're all dressed up," I say. It sounds like I am accusing her of something even worse than not taking me out for yummy Chinese food, a meal that I thought about all the way through a not-so-great week at Oak Glen Primary School. The school she made me go to, by the way.

I used to go to Magdalena School, which was private, girls only. Well, it still *is* private and girls only, I guess. But I'm not going there now. My mom lost her job in San Diego, and last summer we moved to a condo—which is not as good as a house, I don't care what anyone says.

Now my mom looks nervous. She wipes an invisible lipstick smudge from the corner of her mouth and slides her gaze away from mine. *Lipstick!*

"Where are you going, anyway?" I ask, scowling.

"Out for dinner, Emma," Mom tells me. "With a friend."

"What friend?" I ask. "Why can't I come, too?"

"Because—"

"I won't talk," I promise. "I'll just eat, that's all. *Slippery shrimp.*" My mouth waters just saying the words.

"Don't interrupt me again, young lady," Mom says, raising her warning finger.

"Okay," I mumble. "But why can't I go out with you guys? How come I have to go over to Anthony's house?"

"Because I'm going on a date, that's why," my mother blurts out.

She *confesses.*

I am outraged. "A date?" I say. "But—but you're already married, Mom!"

"I—am—not," Mom says, almost biting off the words. "Your father and I have been divorced for more than four years, Emma. And what's more, you know perfectly well that your father got remarried two years ago. To Annabelle. In England."

"I don't know it *perfectly* well," I say, trying to sound calm. "Nothing's perfect, Mom. Like you always say. And maybe Annabelle doesn't even count."

"Now, how do you figure that?" Mom asks, as if she really wants to know.

"They eloped," I say, spelling it out for her. "So we didn't even get to go to the wedding. We don't have any *proof.*"

"Well," Mom says, "I agree that *you* should have been there, Emma. But I'm not all that sorry I missed it." Now she is even smiling a little.

"And anyway," I say, trying to ignore the smile, "I don't believe in divorce."

I heard Cynthia Harbison's mom say this once—to a couple of mothers in front of school. She sounded pretty sure of herself.

"I never used to believe in divorce either," my mom snaps back. "Nevertheless, I'm here to tell you that it exists whether I want it to or not."

I am a little scared of how angry she looks. Who is she mad at, though? Me? My dad?

Annabelle?

Divorce?

My mom scoops me into a hug. "Look, Emma," she says, her voice muffled by my tangly brown hair, which will never look like TV hair in a hundred years. "This is just one Friday night. There will be plenty of others. And you always have fun with Anthony."

"Yeah, but he can be extremely *aggravating*, Mom," I inform her.

"Oh, Emma," Mom says, laughing. "Where did you come from, sweetie?"

"San Diego," I tell her a little sourly. "Remember?"

Mom shakes her head and sighs. "Well, grab your puffy jacket," she says, glancing at her watch. "We can look at some pretty Christmas lights on the way to Anthony's house, if you hurry. I think that big house on the corner finally got those funny-looking reindeer hoisted up onto the roof."

"I wish *we* still had a house," I grumble. "I wish *we* had funny-looking reindeer."

"Don't start in on that," my mother says, raising her warning finger again. "You know perfectly well we never got around to putting up decorations even when we *did* have a house."

"Not *perfectly* well," I say again. "Nothing's perfect, Mom."

"You're telling me," my mom says, laughing some more.

℀ 2 ℀

αɴᴛʜᴏɴʏ ᴛʜᴇ Bᴀʀʙᴀʀɪαɴ

"My mother is on a date," I tell Anthony gloomily, trying out the word—not that my mom's so-called social life is any of his business. I am sitting amid what looks like a sea of LEGOs on his bedroom floor. Anthony Scarpetto has toys in boxes he hasn't even opened yet! And he has a million relatives, *and* a mom and a dad who are still married to each other, and everybody loves him.

I guess people love me, too, only they're scattered all over the world.

Well, scattered all over London, England.

"A date? Like Barbie?" Anthony asks, interested. His brown eyes sparkle.

"Yeah," I say. "Except Barbie isn't real."

"She is *too* real," Anthony tells me. "Natalie at school has one. I seen it."

"'I *saw* it,'" I say, correcting him.

"So you *know* Barbie's real," he says, probably wondering why I am arguing with him.

Spend five minutes with Anthony and you too will feel like you just walked into a wall.

"Can you take this apart?" he asks, giving up on the mysterious LEGO lump he has been wrestling with so hard that his plump cheeks are even pinker than usual. "I need the blue one in the middle," he says, pointing to it.

"They're all the same shape, Anthony," I tell him wearily.

"*Ant*," he says.

"What?" I ask, trying to pry apart the LEGOs, which seem to be stuck together with glue. Or oatmeal.

"My name's Ant, now," he says, sneaking a look at me out of the corner of his eye to see how

I am taking this stupendous news. "We all have nicknames in Miss Becky's class," he adds, trying to sound grown-up.

"What about Natalie?" I say, still working on the stuck LEGOs.

He frowns, suspicious. "How do you know Natalie?" he asks.

"You just told me about her," I say. "And *she* doesn't have a nickname."

"Yes she does," Anthony says. "Natalie *is* her nickname. Her real name's Nat."

"Gnat?" I say, wasting a joke on him. But gnats are very interesting insects. More interesting than you'd think! They do not eat after they are larvae. They only live long enough to lay their eggs and die.

A swarm of gnats is called a ghost.

That would be kind of like kids never eating anything after middle school, not even pizza or French fries. Poor gnats.

"Nat," Anthony repeats, nodding.

I try to figure out how to explain nicknames to him. "A nickname is usually shorter than a person's name," I finally say. "Unless you're someone like Conan the Barbarian, and then it's longer. But 'Pete' is a nickname for 'Peter,' for example. And 'Liz' is short for 'Elizabeth.'"

"Maybe I could be 'Ant' for short, and 'Anthony the Barbarian' for long," Anthony suggests, sounding a little shy.

"That nickname's already been taken by Conan," I tell him.

Anthony sighs. "So what's *your* nickname?" he asks.

"I don't have one."

"I'll give you one," Anthony says. "For free!" He's a generous little guy, in a weird way.

"No thanks," I say. "What's for dinner, do you know?" I ask, trying to change the subject. "Is it slippery shrimp, by any chance?"

Dinner smells more like macaroni and cheese, cheese being one of Anthony's favorite food groups, but a person can always hope.

"Slippery *shrimp?*" Anthony asks, and he starts to laugh. "Yeah, Emma—like that's a real thing people eat!"

"They do eat slippery shrimp," I tell him. "It's

Chinese food, Anthony. Which means Chinese people eat it all the time."

"Slippery *Chinese* shrimp. Oh, sure," Anthony says, still laughing. He shakes his curly black head like the world's youngest geezer. "There's no such thing, Emma. *The End.*"

Anthony has started saying "The End" lately, when he wants something to be over. I think he got it from books.

"Forget I said anything," I tell him just as the gummy LEGOs pop apart. "There," I say, handing him the blue one. *"Now* are you happy?"

"I was happy before, even," Anthony says. "I've been happy ever since my mom said you were coming over to play tonight."

"Oh, Anthony," I say, melting a little.

"Ant," he reminds me patiently. "Call me Ant, okay? Just for tonight? And I'll call you Em."

"Please don't," I tell him, but it's too late. The mind of Anthony Scarpetto has already hopped

ahead to something else. Now, he is busily peeling some unknown goo off the bottom of his red
sneaker.

Yick.

"Okay," I murmur, shuddering. "Call me Em,
if you have to. But just for tonight," I say, echoing
his earlier words.

And, looking at the goo, I start wondering
how my mom's date is going right about now—
but then I make myself stop.

"The End," I whisper to myself.

⅍ 3 ⅍

NucLear acid

"Watch out, Emma! We're a train, and you're standing right on the track," a boy's hoarse voice behind me yells when I am almost in front of Oak Glen Primary School. It is Monday morning. I walk to school, because our condo on Candelaria Road is only six blocks away.

Corey Robinson is the boy who is yelling. He's afraid of arithmetic, but he is a champion swimmer already, even though we're only in the third grade. Sometimes his blond hair turns green when they put too much chlorine in the pool where he trains.

"Yeah," another boy's voice calls out. "And

there's dangerous stuff on board." It's Stanley Washington, who is usually a cautious kind of guy. Like EllRay Jakes, he says "Present" instead of "Here" sometimes, when Ms. Sanchez takes attendance. It always gets a laugh, but we're pretty easy to entertain in Ms. Sanchez's class. Epecially first thing in the morning.

"It's nuclear acid," EllRay roars, bringing up the rear of the imaginary train. I guess he's supposed to be the caboose.

As I have said before, EllRay is little in size but large in noise.

"There's no such thing as nuclear acid," I shout after them as they *whoop-whoop-whoop* their way up the concrete steps that lead to the front hallway where the school offices are.

Boys like yelling in hallways because they're so nice and echo-y. (The halls are nice and echo-y, not the boys.) Another thing about boys is that they're extra brave when there's a whole bunch of them together, like now. But if I bumped into Corey or Stanley or EllRay on the playground, and whoever-it-was was alone, he wouldn't be yelling "nuclear acid" at me and be expecting me to get out of his way, that's for sure.

Well, I guess girls are the same, being braver in groups than they are when they're alone. Not that a girl would invent something like nuclear acid as a way of having fun. That's pure boy.

I stand in front of the school under the pepper tree and wait for my friend Annie Pat Masterson to arrive, being careful not to step on any nuclear acid that might have spilled on the sidewalk, ha ha. It was supposed to start raining last night, only it didn't. All that rain is still waiting somewhere up in the sky, which means that the air will just get heavier and heavier until something finally happens.

Like—*ka-boom!*

Meanwhile, most of us kids will be either too hot or too cold today, depending on what wrong thing we wore to school. And in addition to the almost-bad weather, it's Monday, which makes everything worse—for kids *and* for teachers, probably.

Monday is bad the way Friday is good, when you're in primary school.

"I'm freezing," Annie Pat Masterson says ten seconds after joining me under the pepper tree. Every so often, a tiny red berry plonks down onto our heads, and we shake it off, fast, just in case it's an insect and not a berry.

Annie Pat is wearing skinny jeans today, and a red turtleneck shirt, and a pullover sweater that matches her navy-blue eyes perfectly. Her red pigtails—not the same color red as the turtleneck—

look extra springy in the damp morning air. She shivers, demonstrating how cold she is.

"Well, I'm too hot," I say, adjusting my puffy pink jacket so that some cool air seeps down my neck.

"But I'm *just right*," a chirpy, confident voice says as its owner comes skipping up behind us.

It's Cynthia Harbison—doing her Goldilocks imitation, I guess. Cynthia is a girl who's perfect every day, in every way.

Except she's not a very good friend. I learned that the hard way. Cynthia will talk about you behind your back—or to your face—just to stir things up when she's bored, or to make herself interesting. And she hardly ever gets in trouble for it.

For Cynthia Harbison, crime pays.

She does look "just right" today, however. She is wearing a short, faded denim jacket over T-shirts layered so carefully that their bottom hems seem to make little ribbons of color around her hips.

And she is wearing jeans that flare out perfectly at the bottom.

"Hi, Cynthia," Annie Pat says, but Cynthia is already long gone and up the stairs, heading toward Heather and Fiona, her loyal sidekicks, who are waiting by the school's front door. Each of those two girls is okay on her own, I have learned, but they change for the worse when they're together—or, for sure, when they're with Cynthia.

The only girl in our class who gets along well with everyone is Krysten "Kry" Rodriguez, who started school late this year. Kry isn't even here yet. She's really pretty, but she's not stuck-up about it.

I hate to admit it, but I think I might be stuck-up a little, if I were that pretty. But I would be *kind.*

"Want to go hang out on the playground?" I ask Annie Pat. "There's still ten minutes before school starts. I'll let you wear my jacket," I add, before she can tell me it's too cold to play outside.

"But what'll *you* wear?" Annie Pat asks.

"I'll be okay," I say bravely, steering her toward the chain link gate. "I have to tell you something important. But you have to promise not to tell anyone."

"Okay," Annie Pat says, her eyes wide. She pokes her arms down into my jacket's pre-warmed sleeves and waits patiently. The cold sinks into my sweaty, long-sleeved T-shirt like icewater, but I just stand there, trying to figure out where to start.

"Cross my heart and hope to die," Annie Pat says, quoting the old promise, and so I start talking before she gets to the part that goes, *"And stick a needle in my eye."* Because—yow!

"My-mom-went-out-on-a-date-last-Friday-night," I say, speaking as fast as I can. I peek around to see if anyone else is listening in, but so far, so good.

"Huh? Say that again, Emma," Annie Pat tells me. "Only slower this time."

"My mother went out on a *date*," I repeat, hating the words.

"Cool," Annie Pat says, her navy-blue eyes shining with the so-called romance of it all. "Was the man handsome? Did he bring her candy and flowers?"

"I didn't meet him," I tell her. "I don't even know his name."

Annie Pat's eyes grow wide. "So it could be *anybody*?"

"Anybody in Oak Glen," I say, narrowing it down a little. "And don't look so happy about it, Annie Pat. Because this is a disaster. It's—it's *nuclear acid*."

Annie Pat's brow wrinkles. She wants to be a scientist when she grows up, too, and she probably knows there isn't any such thing.

"I mean it's *like* nuclear acid," I say quickly. "It's nuclear acid–*ish*."

"But—why?" Annie Pat asks, still frowning a little as she decides not to challenge me about the acid. "Maybe he's nice?" she says cautiously, making it a question.

"He is *not* nice," I say fiercely.

And because Annie Pat is my friend, she slowly nods her head in agreement. "Not nice," she echoes as we walk to class.

My brain feels as though it is pounding inside my skull.

And I think I may be getting a stomachache, too.

Thanks, *Mom*.

✗ 4 ✗

Word Search

While Ms. Sanchez takes attendance, I look out the window at the cloudy sky. I squint at the trees and try to tell if it is raining yet—because I already know I'm "Here." Or "Present," as EllRay or Stanley will probably say when Ms. Sanchez calls their names. So I don't have to pay attention.

Ms. Sanchez always wears her shiny black hair pulled back into a bun, but on her it looks good. She uses her engagement hand a lot when she is explaining things, because she likes to watch her ring sparkle. Ms. Sanchez is engaged to marry Mr. Timberlake—not the famous one who's on TV all the time, even though he's still handsome—but we don't know when the wedding will be.

I secretly wish I could be her flower girl.

They are going to live happily ever after. Somebody has to.

Ms. Sanchez is wearing very pretty colors today, probably to cheer herself up because of the weather: a coral sweater, which Annie Pat will really like because she wants to be a marine biologist, and real coral is alive and lives under the sea, and dark chocolate-colored boots, which *I* really like because—*mmm*, chocolate.

Ms. Sanchez wears such cute outfits! In fact, Fiona McNulty has started a secret fashion notebook where she draws what our teacher is wearing each day.

I think Ms. Sanchez dresses so nicely because she's in love. But Annie Pat and I have promised each other that even if we never fall in love, we will wear cute clothes when we grow up, just like Ms. Sanchez does. We will never dress the way our moms do, in baby-spitty turtlenecks and pull-on pants—like Annie Pat's mother, because of Annie Pat's baby brother, Murphy—or in pull-overs, jeans, and boring flat sandals, which my mom wears, because she works at home.

Scientists can look as cute as anyone, we have decided. And they can wear extremely high heels.

"I have a word-search activity paper for you to do this morning," Ms. Sanchez announces, sur-prising us—because activity papers are almost like games. They're usually for rainy Friday after-noons, not Monday mornings, when you're sup-posed to work like crazy to make up for having relaxed your brain all weekend. "And it's dinosaur themed," Ms. Sanchez adds, which makes the boys in our class very happy.

"*Yes!*" Corey whispers, pumping his fist in the air. He sits next to me.

Jared Matthews glares at him, then sits up im-portantly in his seat, because dinosaurs are "his thing," as he likes to tell everyone. It is obvious that Jared intends to be the best dinosaur word-search kid in our class.

Jared's *real* thing is being a bully, in my opin-ion, and bossing smaller kids around—which means just about everyone, because he is so huge. Jared has swirly brown hair, large hands, and lots of freckles.

Annie Pat and I are a little scared of Jared, be-cause he has a very bad temper.

Not this morning, though! This morning,

Jared is all smiles. He grabs his word-search paper eagerly and scrabbles in his desk for his yellow highlighter pen.

"And—you may begin," Ms. Sanchez says, sinking into her desk chair. She starts correcting a stack of papers.

I look down at the list of words at the bottom of my word search. Some of the words, like *Jurassic*, *carnivore*, and *herbivore*, are about dinosaurs, and some of the words—*Triceratops*, *Allosaurus*, and *Raptor*—are the names of dinosaurs.

But I can't concentrate. *"Cool. Is he handsome?"* Annie Pat had said when I told her about my mom's date.

I look at the big square block of letters that form the word search, and my headache starts to pound again, and my stomach churns. Were those the only four words Annie Pat could think of to say? She didn't get it at all!

"Stop daydreaming, Emma," Ms. Sanchez says, glancing over at me.

```
C  L  O  P  I  S  O  L  M  G  A
A  J  R  R  A  P  T  O  R  R  L
R  F  U  S  Q  U  H  N  O  E  L
N  H  E  R  B  I  V  O  R  E  O
I  O  G  C  A  F  Z  D  A  N  S
V  V  B  Y  I  S  J  U  N  O  A
O  O  N  A  H  L  S  B  C  P  U
R  I  G  N  E  G  D  I  E  Y  R
E  X  T  I  N  C  T  W  C  K  U
T  R  I  C  E  R  A  T  O  P  S
```

DINOSAURS

JURASSIC   CARNIVORE
HERBIVORE   EXTINCT
TRICERATOPS   ALLOSAURUS
RAPTOR

So I look at my word search again. The letters all blur together, though, and they do not start forming any of the given words at all. But next to me, Corey is drawing wavy yellow lines up and down, back and forth across his block of letters, and he's gleefully checking off words at the bottom of the page.

Check.

Check.

Check!

And Jared seems to be working even faster than Corey.

So I start drawing a yellow line through anything that even *looks* like a word. *Lopisol, greenop,* and *nodub. Oonah, rigneg,* and *rorance.*

Corey glances over at my paper and begins to look nervous.

Hey, this is fun! It's so much fun that I start to giggle, and Corey shoots me a dirty look. Now he is falling further behind Jared.

But I don't even care. Maybe Ms. Sanchez will ask me to use my words in a sentence. "The *greenop* grazed in the *rorance* forest, until the *nodub lopisol* came along and ate him right before the meteor hit," I'll tell everyone, just as if it really happened.

And how can anyone say it *didn't* happen? Do people actually think that Triceratops *knew* they were called Triceratops? Maybe they thought of themselves as *greenops*, instead.

"Emma?" a voice behind me says.

Wow! How did Ms. Sanchez sneak up behind me?

I try to hide my fake words from her eyes.

"I'd like to talk to you for a minute, please, Miss *Lopisol*," she murmurs. "In the back of the room. Eyes on your papers, people," she calls out to the kids who are now staring at me: Annie Pat, who is looking worried, and EllRay, who is looking sympathetic, and Cynthia, whose eyes are shining with excitement.

Jackals are omnivores— they'll eat nearly anything!

Sometimes Cynthia Harbison reminds me of a jackal. My favorite nature book says that jackals are "opportunistic carnivores." I think that means they'll pounce on any animal that's down—

like Cynthia does with me—and then *eat* it.

I slink to the back of the class, behind Ms. Sanchez. She takes me gently by the shoulder. "What's up, Emma?" she says, which reminds me so much of that cartoon guy Elmer Fudd for a second that I start to giggle again. I think I'm nervous.

"Sorry," I say, trying to make my mouth obey me and stop laughing.

Ms. Sanchez scowls—and she's *still* pretty. "This is not funny, Emma," she tells me. "You're not acting at all like yourself today."

She's right! She's right! Because I am *not* myself today. I am a girl whose father lives in England and whose mother is now dating a strange man.

Which leaves me *all alone*, in case you didn't notice. I'm practically an orphan!

I try to find the words that will make Ms. Sanchez like me again, without me having to tell her my private business. "I'm sorry. But—my stomach hurts," I say, clutching at my middle.

Ta-da! I have instantly turned a small worry-

ache in my stomach into what Ms. Sanchez must be thinking are sharp, stabbing pains, with the possible forecast of hurling in the immediate future, and I feel only a little bit guilty.

"I think I'd better go home," I add, my voice weak. "Before I—*you* know."

Before I *vomit*, I add silently. Before I *vomit*, Ms. Sanchez! All over your cute brown boots!

I don't say this last part out loud, but I don't have to. Teachers everywhere hate it when a student throws up in class, because then they have to take care of the sick kid *and* wait for the custodian with the sawdust at the same time. Also, one or two other kids in class are sure to start gagging, just thinking about what happened.

Vomiting can be contagious—like yawning, only a hundred times worse, because yawning never involves a custodian with sawdust.

Ms. Sanchez has already stepped back a couple of paces, probably to protect her boots. "I'll call the school nurse and tell her you're coming," she says in a great big hurry.

"Can't you just call my mom?" I ask in a wheedly, about-to-barf way. "She's home. She *works* at home."

"That'll be up to the nurse," Ms. Sanchez tells me. "Now, go gather your things, Emma. Remember to get your jacket from the closet, too. And I hope we see you back here soon, honey. *Feel better.*"

And do you know what?

I already do!

x 5 x

Happily Ever Emma

"Of course you're well enough to go back to school tomorrow," my mom tells me right after dinner. "Look at what you just ate, for heaven's sake."

Meatballs, mashed potatoes, and peas. And applesauce for dessert.

Sure, I ate everything. But maybe I was only being polite.

"In my humble opinion," Mom says, "you were well enough *today* to stay in school." She gives me a look. "The nurse said so, Emma. In fact, I don't know why I let you talk me into bringing you home. I figured you needed a day off, so I gave in. But don't press your luck, sweetie."

"I *did* need a day off," I agree. "And about that so-called school nurse, I don't think she really even is one! She doesn't wear a uniform, Mom. Just regular clothes. And she keeps saying 'tummy,' instead of 'stomach,' which is just *wrong*, if you're a real nurse. Sure, she has a stethoscope and a name tag, but that doesn't make it official. Anyone can buy those things in a costume store."

Mom laughs. "So you think the school nurse is pulling off some elaborate stunt because she really, really, really wants little kids to sneeze on her all day long? And upchuck in her office?"

"Hey, I just ate," I remind my mom, cradling my stomach—which really could still be queasy, for all she knows.

But I do think it's funny how my mom says "upchuck." What a weird word. It reminds me of *woodchuck*. Did you know that a woodchuck is the same thing as a groundhog? And that woodchucks

Woodchucks whistle to alert other woodchucks to danger.

are mostly vegetarians, and by the end of October they are fast asleep under the ground—for the entire winter? Sounds okay to me, the way things are going.

"You will be at school tomorrow," Mom says slowly. She gives one last wipe to the kitchen counter with a Santa Claus dish towel and then throws the towel into an almost-full laundry basket.

Then she tosses her library book into the basket, too. "I'll be downstairs doing the wash," she says in her coolest voice. "Remember, Emma, don't open the front door to anyone, *no matter what.*"

We usually do the laundry together on Saturday morning, not Monday night, so it is clear that my mom is just trying to get away from me for a while.

"But what if there's an emergency?" I ask, trying to sound pathetic. "I won't be able to call you. You lost your cell phone, remember?"

"*You* lost it, Emma, and there won't be an emergency. But if there is, start yelling, and I'll hear you. Or dial nine-one-one."

"What if I get hungry?"

"In the next *hour*?" Mom asks, smiling. "Eat some fruit, Emma. You have my permission. Live it up."

"What if I get scared?"

"Turn on all the lights. Or call Annie Pat. Look, Emma," my mother says, leaning forward to make sure I hear each word. "It's not as if I'm taking off for Las Vegas. I will just be down one flight of stairs and around the corner, in our condominium's laundry room. You've been half-a-step away from me all day long, ever since you talked your way home from school this morning. So I really need some time alone with a washing machine, a dryer, and a good book. Understand?"

"No," I mumble. Because I will *never* understand

why my mom doesn't want to be with me every single minute of every single day. Until last Friday, I thought she did.

Me, and only me! We were going to live happily ever Emma.

I mean happily ever *after.*

This is all the fault of that date.

"Good," Mom says, which proves she wasn't listening to me.

x x x

I'm not really afraid of being almost alone for an hour, even when it's dark outside. Oak Glen is a safe place to live, and Candelaria is a quiet street, and our condo is packed with people—mostly old—who peek out of their windows when anyone even tiptoes by. But it makes me feel nervous when my very own mom acts like it's a chore just being around me.

I try to go over my spelling list, but how can you practice spelling words all by yourself?

Luckily, I can stop even trying, because the kitchen phone is ringing. *Brrr-rrr!* "Hi, A.P.," I say, picking up the receiver—because I am sure it is Annie Pat calling to tell me how wrong my mom was for going on that date.

"Hello," an unfamiliar man's voice says. "Is Maggie there?"

Maggie is my mom: Margaret "Maggie" McGraw.

It's that man she went out with. I'm sure of it!

My brain is suddenly flooded with choices. *One*, I could just hang up, or *two*, I could pretend I only speak some strange foreign language, or *three*, I could say he has the wrong number and *then* hang up, or *four*, I could say that my mother doesn't want to talk to him ever again, or *five*, I could say, *"She can't come to the phone right now,"* and then take a message, which is what I'm supposed to do if my mom happens to be busy when somebody calls.

Usually, she's in the bathroom when I say, *"She can't come to the phone."*

Every kid knows that you never say, *"My mother is gone, gone, gone! And who knows when she'll be back? I am all alone here, and totally unprotected!"* when some stranger calls on the phone.

I don't have the nerve to choose numbers one, two, three, or four, so I panic and choose number five, which my mom would say was the right choice to make. "I'm sorry, but Maggie can't come to the phone right now. May I take a message?" I look around for paper and a pencil. I can't find either, but who cares? It's not like I'm really gonna write anything down.

"Is this Emma?" the voice asks, all friendly and jolly.

He knows my name after *one*

date with my mom? This is too much!

"It all depends," I tell him in my frostiest voice.

"Well, okay," he says, sounding a little confused. "This is Dennis Engelman. And it's a complicated message, so I'll go slowly. Are you ready to write it all down?"

"Sure," I say, trying to hold the phone and peel a banana—fruit, Mom!—at the same time. I also practice winking one eye, which makes the clock on the wall seem to jump back and forth. Cool.

"It's about this coming Wednesday night," he tells me slowly, so I can supposedly get every detail of the message right. "I can't make it up to Oak Glen that night after all. My out-of-town client is arriving in San Diego a day early, and I'm going to have to take him out for a big seafood dinner. So I have to cancel my date with your mom."

Awww.

"But I'm hoping we can change our date to Friday," the man—Dennis Engelman—continues. "Maybe we can meet at that Italian restaurant she likes in Escondido. At, say, seven thirty. And you're welcome to join us, Emma. If this is Miss Emma McGraw to whom I am speaking," he adds in a jokey way, speaking like someone in an old movie.

"I'm writing it all down," I fib, not giving anything away.

The man sighs. "So ask Maggie to call me at home tonight if there's a problem with the change, okay? Or if she just wants to talk," he adds, sounding a little lonely all of a sudden.

"Sure. Okey-dokey. I'll tell her," I say through a mouthful of banana—because this strange-man-who-knows-my-name does not deserve my very best manners.

And he is *not* going to have a second date with my mom.

"Thanks," the man says. "Well, good-bye, young lady. Whoever you are!"

"Bye," I say, and I hang up the phone as hard as I possibly can.

❊ ❊ ❊

My mother is a lot calmer than before when she comes back upstairs from doing the laundry. "How's the homework coming, Emma?" she asks, balancing the laundry basket on one hip. "Were there any phone calls?" She sounds shy.

Aha! So she *thought* he might call. And she didn't even tell me about going out next Wednesday night. She was going to spring it on me!

"Nope," I say, feeling only a little bit guilty. "My homework's finished, and it's been pretty quiet, except for when I ate a banana. Can I watch TV before bedtime?"

"For half an hour," Mom says, nodding. "If we can agree on the show. And then you can read in bed a little, and then it's nighty-night, sleep tight."

"Nighty-night," I agree, looking away. "Sleep tight."

Maybe *Dennis Engelman* won't sleep tight tonight, though—because Mom's not going to call him, no matter how lonely he is.

℀ 6 ℀

Guilt Sandwich

"Did he sound tall, Emma?" Annie Pat asks me the next day, Tuesday, during lunch.

"How does a person sound tall? That doesn't even make any sense," I say. A cool breeze ruffles my curly brown hair, and Annie Pat's pigtails quiver. I take a bite of my bagel sandwich.

"Well, what about handsome? Did he sound *handsome?*" she persists, nipping off the corner of her tuna sandwich and looking at me with her navy-blue eyes.

My friend Annie Pat is very romantic. She is trying to remain loyal to me by not liking the man my mom went out with on a date, but at the same time, she wants that man to be wonderful.

"Did *who* sound handsome?" Kry Rodriguez says, plopping down next to me on the bench and opening her lunchbox, which she decorated herself with stickers and sequins. And it looks great, that's how cool Kry is.

I wanted this talk with Annie Pat to be private, but we both like Kry a lot. Kry is fun to be with *and* to look at, because her shiny black hair falls over her shoulders like a waterfall. Also, Kry's bangs are so long that Annie Pat sometimes wonders how she can see. But I know that Kry can see perfectly well—the way Yorkshire Terriers can see, even though their long, silky fur may be flopping way over their eyes.

Spread your fingers apart, hold your hand in front of your face, and then stare through your open fingers at something in the distance. That's what it must be like for hairy dogs, and for Kry.

Annie Pat nudges my ribs with her elbow and looks sideways at me, silently asking whether she should answer Kry—because this whole thing about my mom going on a date is supposed to be a deep dark secret.

But what Annie Pat doesn't know is that I am keeping some things secret even from *her*. For instance, I did not tell her about Dennis needing to cancel his date with my mother on Wednesday night. And I didn't tell Annie Pat that he is expecting my mom to meet him for dinner at an Italian restaurant in Escondido on Friday.

Of course, I didn't tell my mother those things, either, which will make Wednesday night at our house bad, bad, bad for my mom, and Friday night at the restaurant extremely strange and sad for Dennis.

I *hope*. Because maybe then he'll give up.

But all this drama is giving me an unfamiliar, funny feeling inside, somewhere between my stomach and my throat. Is this what guilt feels like?

Hey, Annie Pat is sitting on one side of me, and Kry is on the other, and I am stuck in the middle. It's a guilt sandwich! Because Annie Pat and Kry are really nice, the way I used to be.

I still think I did the right thing about that phone call, though. But even if I didn't, it's too late to make it right. And it's not as if I told my mom a big fat lie. I just didn't tell her one small skinny truth, that's all.

"Is *who* handsome?" Kry asks patiently.

I decide that I might feel better if I tell Kry some of what has been happening. After all, her mom is divorced, too, so maybe she'll understand. "My mother went out on a date with some random guy a week ago," I say, trying to say it in a way that is fair, but that will make Kry see everything my way. "And she just *shouldn't* have, that's all. But her date called last night when Mom was downstairs doing the laundry, and I forgot to give her the message. Only it's for her own good," I add, believing the words the second I say them.

It *is* for my mother's own good—because look at how miserable she was when she got divorced! I was only four years old, but even I could tell that she was pretty sad. She cried a lot, and she forgot how to have fun for a long time, and she told her friends she couldn't talk about it, and then she talked to them about it on the phone for hours.

It was *boring*.

She even packed the wrong day-care snack for me—more than once, too.

How could she even *think* of dating again?

"Whoa," Kry says, her sandwich frozen halfway to her mouth. "You'd better tell her he called, Emma," she advises. "You have to tell grown-ups when they get a phone message, or—or—"

"Or an emergency could happen," Annie Pat

says, her eyes wide as she finishes Kry's sentence.

"Yeah," Kry agrees, nodding solemnly. "And you might not be allowed to answer the phone any more."

"Who cares?" I say, shrugging. "It rings too much anyway."

Kry sighs. "I wish *my* mom would start dating again," she announces to Annie Pat and me.

"No you don't," I tell her.

"Yes I do," Kry says, rummaging in her lunch box for something good to eat. "Maybe it would cheer her up a little."

If Kry says something, it's because she means it, so I give up.

Annie Pat nods slightly, as if agreeing with Kry about how Mrs. Rodriguez should start dating again.

They agree! It's two against one.

Now, I *really* can't tell Annie Pat and Kry the details about my mom's date tomorrow night, and

the next-Friday date, and how neither one is going to happen, thanks to me.

I feel lonely, even though I am the only right person in the entire world.

And I still have that bad feeling stuck somewhere between my stomach and my throat.

But maybe it's just a piece of my bagel sandwich.

x 7 x

a Bad Night on Candelaria Road

It is a wet Wednesday afternoon, and I am walk-
ing home from school as slowly as I can without
going backward. I stare at people's droopy, drippy
holiday decorations.

Sloths sleep
for 16 to
18 hours
every day.

I pretend I am a sloth, one of the
pokiest animals on earth.

Maybe everything will be okay
tonight, I think, trying hard to cheer
myself up. Maybe Dennis Engelman
called my mom again to remind
her he had to cancel, but magically,
they're not mad at me. Or, if he didn't

call again, maybe Mom is relieved. Maybe—

"Come on, Emma," Annie Pat says from some-where under the hood of her shiny pink raincoat. "Can't you walk any faster?"

The rain patters down on my own hood. (I wear a slicker because I always lose umbrellas.) "Nope," I tell her gloomily. "You go on ahead."

"Okay," Annie Pat says. "But only because I have to. My mom is waiting for me so we can take Murphy to the doctor. He has an *appointment*," she says, making it sound like a big deal—as if her little brother is the president of some bank, and not just an ordinary baby. "The toothless wonder," Annie Pat and I have started calling him.

He is pretty cute, though, with his little tufts of red hair and his crazy gummy smile.

"Bye," I call out, because Annie Pat is already skipping down the sidewalk toward her own street, Sycamore Lane, which is two blocks past my street, Candelaria Road.

Except Annie Pat has a house, not a condo, *and* she has a baby brother, *and* two parents who stayed married. Also, as far as I know, she doesn't have a guilty conscience about *anything*.

Some kids have all the luck.

x x x

"I'm home," I whisper as I close our front door behind me.

"Emma," Mom exclaims from down the hall,

and I am horrified to see her rush into the living room wearing a bathrobe and a towel wrapped like a turban around her head.

This means she just washed her hair, which is something she usually does in the morning—unless it's a special occasion.

Oh, no. She is getting all fixed up for her canceled date tonight!

"Where have you been?" Mom asks, looking at an imaginary watch on her still-damp wrist. "I expected you half an hour ago. I was getting worried!"

"I'm sorry," I say, dropping my backpack onto the floor and peeling off my crayon-yellow slicker. "Annie Pat had to stay late at school," I explain, making up the lie on the spot.

Telling it doesn't seem too bad, though, compared to what I did on Monday night. Or what I *didn't* do—which was to tell my mom that Dennis Engelman called.

And that he's not coming tonight.

Being bad seems to get easier once you've already started, especially if you get away with it the first time.

I guess I'm big bad Emma these days.

"Well, you're here now, at least," Mom says, rubbing her sticking-out hair with the towel. "Grab a snack, sweetie, and get started on your homework. Because—surprise! There's a really fun sitter coming, and if you've finished all your work, you guys can watch TV together."

"A *sitter?*" I yelp, because ever since we moved to Oak Glen, I have always gone over to Annie Pat's house, or Anthony Scarpetto's, whenever my mom has had to do something alone.

"That's right," my mother says, nodding. "And you're finally going to get to meet my friend Dennis Engelman tonight, Emma. I decided it's time. Then he and I have dinner plans. And since it's a school night, I figured you'd be better off staying home with a sitter, so you could get your work done and get to bed on time."

"But—who's coming?" I ask in a croaky voice, because we have lived in Oak Glen for more than four months, and like I said, I have never had an at-home sitter. Not once. I am too old and too mature for an official sitter, in my opinion. Anyway, what did Mom do? Go out on the street and ask the first stranger she met to come over tonight and watch TV with me?

"Who's the sitter?" I ask again, barely squeezing out the words.

"Her name's Shayna," my mom says happily. "And she and her family live downstairs. She's in high school, Emma, and she's just adorable. I met her in the laundry room last Monday night."

I can't even move. I just stare at my mom.

Mom still thinks Dennis Engelman is coming over tonight to take her out.

And she wants to "finally" introduce us—after just one date!

But he isn't coming, because he's feeding seafood to a visitor in San Diego.

And Mom won't know what to think when he doesn't show up.

And there's going to be an adorable witness to this entire disaster.

I don't know what was going on in my brain at the time, but when I didn't give my mother that phone message on Monday night, I never dreamed I'd get caught. I guessed that Mom would say, "Oh well, good riddance!" when Dennis Engelman didn't appear tonight, and I figured Dennis Engelman would want to forget all about my mom when she stood him up next Friday. I thought things would get back to normal around here. I never planned on *this.*

It's going to be a bad night on Candelaria Road.

And on top of everything else, there is no *way* I can keep from getting in trouble when they figure out what I did. Or, rather, what I *didn't.*

"Get a move on, Emma," my mom says, laughing.

"Okay," I say, and I plod into the kitchen for

my after-school snack, which I barely manage to choke down.

"Wow, this is pretty harsh," Shayna whispers to me two and a half hours later. "Your mom's date is more than an hour late. And she bought a new pink dress, too."

Shayna *is* really cute, and she's also very nice. She brought a stack of celebrity magazines that we are looking at together, which is a privilege, since she knows so much about famous people. And we are watching TV at the same time.

It is the exact opposite of my normal everyday life.

This would be so extremely cool—if it weren't so terrible! Because Shayna's right. Mom is sitting all alone in the kitchen, waiting for Dennis Engelman to show up and take her out for dinner, and he is probably still eating shrimp cocktail

in San Diego. Or maybe he and his business guy are eating dessert by now. Extra-fancy hot fudge sundaes.

"Why doesn't she just call him again?" Shayna asks, keeping her voice low. Her forehead is wrinkled with concern for my mom. "Maybe he finally turned his cell on. That jerk!"

"She won't call him again," I murmur, turning a magazine page with cold fingers. "My mom's not exactly the type to keep calling someone up over and over." Especially not a *man*, I add silently, because Mom is pretty old-fashioned in a lot of ways.

"Well, *I'd* call him, if that was me sitting in the kitchen, and I'd tell him where to get off, too," Shayna whispers, furious on my mom's behalf. She whips her caramel-colored ponytail around like she is getting ready to go into battle.

Shayna sure cares a lot about my mom, and she barely even knows her!

This makes me feel guiltier than ever. Here I am, Mom's *daughter*, who a minute ago was having fun while looking at photographs of famous people. Meanwhile, poor Mom is fidgeting with her brand-new pink dress in the kitchen. And she hardly ever buys new clothes.

Mom probably thinks that Dennis Engelman doesn't care enough about her even to *call*.

I blush with shame, but I still cannot figure out a way to tell my mom the truth.

Epecially not with Shayna here. "Are you *sure* it's a new dress?" I whisper, flipping another page. "Because I think maybe I've seen her wear it before."

"No, it's new, all right," Shayna tells me. "Your mom bought it just for tonight. She told me it was their six-month anniversary, and she wanted to wear something special. Oh, this is messed-*up*."

"She's been seeing Dennis Engelman for six months?" I squawk. "But—but I thought they only went out one time!"

Shayna shakes her head, and her turquoise eyes—contacts?—shine with sympathy for my poor mother. "They've been dating for six months," she says firmly. "And then he just blows her off like this. I don't think she should stand for it," she announces, jumping up from the sofa.

Oh, no! What's she going to do, start offering my mom dating advice? "Wait," I say, tugging at her sleeve. "You'd better stay here, Shayna.

Because—my mom likes to be alone when she's upset."

"Really?" Shayna says, glancing longingly toward the kitchen.

And, as if she's been summoned by magic, my mother is suddenly standing in the living room, holding the phone. The blusher on her cheeks looks like two pink patches on

her white, white face. "I'm calling the police," she announces. "Because there must have been a car accident or something, and that's why Dennis hasn't called."

x **8** x

Short and Sweet

"I'll make this short and sweet," Mom says to me fifteen minutes later, after Shayna has been hustled out the front door with a fistful of money—money that she almost didn't accept.

I will never forget the way Shayna looked at me when I blurted out why Mom should *not* call the police. Or the look my mother gave me, which was even worse.

"I already said I'm sorry," I mumble, not daring to look Mom in the eye.

"I *beg* your pardon?" my mom says, which in Mom-talk means that she cannot believe what she just heard. She is as angry as I have ever seen her.

"Nothing," I say hastily.

"Good answer," Mom snaps. "So, here it is, short and sweet, Emma. I want you to write Dennis a letter of apology—and write one to me, too, while you're at it."

"But I never even met him," I object weakly. "And *he* doesn't know I didn't give you the message. So why do I have to apologize to him?"

"You wouldn't have said a word if I hadn't said I was going to call the police," Mom replies, not really answering my question. "And would it have been okay with you if I'd just cried myself to sleep?"

Hearing her say this, I can barely keep from crying myself. "No. I would have felt *terrible*," I tell her.

"Oh, boo-hoo," my mother says angrily. "But you wouldn't have bothered to tell me that Dennis was expecting me to meet him for dinner this Friday, either, would you?"

"I don't *know-w-w*," I say, my tears finally spill-

ing over. "After Shayna said you were wearing a new dress, I was trying to figure out a way to tell you, only I didn't want to get in trouble!"

"Well, why *shouldn't* you get in trouble when you've done something wrong?" Mom asks, fed up.

I don't have a very good answer to that question. "You don't have to be so *mean*," I finally say, hoping this will trick her into feeling at least a little bit sorry for me.

"Oh, yes I do," my mom says in her most serious voice.

I wish she still liked me.

"Look, Emma," Mom says, sighing. "I don't expect you to be perfect. But when you mess up, you have to say you're sorry—and then do what you can to make things right. You can't just hide your head in the sand."

"Like an ostrich," I say sadly, and incorrectly, because nature scientists say that ostriches don't really do this at all. But I wish I had a pile of sand handy right this very minute. I could start a new tradition for in-trouble eight-year-olds who happen to live in Oak Glen, California.

Ostriches do not bury their heads in the sand—that's just a myth!

Scientists could come study *me*.

"Like an ostrich," Mom agrees. "Because that's just silly, Emma. Also it's not very brave."

Not very brave. That's just a nice way of saying I was a coward.

"Well, you were going out with Dennis Engelman for six whole months," I blurt out, angry and ashamed at the same time. "You told adorable Shayna, and she's a total stranger, but you never told me. And I'm a *relative*. So that wasn't very brave, either."

Mom blushes. "I suppose you're right, in a way. But I wasn't sure Dennis and I were going to keep seeing each other after you and I moved to Oak Glen last summer," she tells me. "We did, though."

"Well, *obviously*," I say with a sniff.

"That's quite enough back talk, young lady," my mom tells me, in charge of things once more. "Now, march into your room and start writing those two letters. And then come show them to me, and I'll tuck you in."

"And give me a kiss good night?" I ask, my voice so soft that I'm surprised she can even hear it.

But she does. "Of course, Emma," Mom says, pulling me to her for a hug. Her new dress is very silky. And she's wearing *perfume*.

"We can start over fresh tomorrow morning," my mom promises me. "Tonight, even."

"I'm sorry, Mommy," I say, nestling my face against her brand-new dress, being careful not to get any tear marks or drool marks on it.

"I know, Emma. Now, scoot."

And so I scoot.

x 9 x

Our Date with Dennis

"Would you like a breadstick, Emma?" Dennis Engelman asks.

It is Friday night, and I am all dressed up and sitting next to my mother—across from Dennis Engelman—in that fancy Italian restaurant in Escondido, California. Yes, he and my mom got together on the phone and decided that this was the best way to "handle things." That's how grownups put it, like there's a handle on top of every problem.

Hah!

This is my worst nightmare come true. On top of that, it could ruin Italian food for me forever. I'll be scarred for life. No more spaghetti and meatballs. No ravioli. No *pizza*.

"I *guess*," I mumble.

"Emma . . ." my mother warns.

"I mean *yes*, thank you," I tell him, grabbing the nearest breadstick, because there's no point in starving, is there? "Please pass the butter," I say gloomily.

My mom fiddles with the fake holly wreath around our table's glowing red candle and exchanges a look with Dennis Engelman that I cannot interpret, then she scoots over a dish filled with foil-wrapped pats of butter. I take three, just in case.

This is what I wish *all* butter looked like, all the time! Because who wants even the possibility of other people's crumbs on their own private food? Besides, butter is prettier this way, all shiny and dressed up.

I unwrap two of my three pats and start piling butter on my breadstick in a long, skinny mountain ridge while Mom and Dennis Engelman watch, silent.

Dennis Engelman *is* tall, Annie Pat will be happy to learn, and even though he wears glasses he is medium-handsome, which I have to admit is just about right for a man. Because what lady wants to go out with someone who looks better than she does? Not that Mom looks bad or anything. She looks beautiful, and she is wearing her

almost-new, silky-soft, pale-pink dress again.

I am wearing my best dress, which is dark green and has long sleeves. Its skirt is so smooth that I keep starting to slide off the dark-red leather seat, so far off that my nose is practically sitting on the table. I can barely eat my breadstick. But it's fun pretending that I'm a Christmas leprechaun.

"Don't slouch, Emma," my mom murmurs, and so I hoist myself back up.

"Okay, but Mr. Engelman dropped his napkin again," I announce to everyone at our table. All three of us.

See, Dennis Engelman's dark pants are *also* kind of smooth, and whenever he leans forward to pass us something, his cloth napkin skids to the floor. He and I are sitting across from each other on the booth's outside seats, so I notice these things.

"Oops," I add, truly surprised, because while noticing Dennis Engelman's napkin *and* trying to hold both the very tall menu and my butter

knife at the same time, I have accidentally spilled my glass of ice water all over the tablecloth. I just barely rescue my breadstick, which suddenly looks like a tiny canoe carrying a load of butter down the Amazon. Or *up* the Amazon, I can never remember which.

"*Emma,*" Mom scolds gently—about the napkin comment, I am sure, and not the spilled water. Dennis Engelman actually blushes a little, then he scoops up his napkin from the restaurant's carpet, which is decorated with crazy orange swirls— probably to hide the spaghetti sauce people have spilled. I bet you could eat down there for a week. He signals for the waiter.

So far, so bad, I think, hiding a mean little smile. Our date with Dennis is going just perfectly! Except the edges of my sleeves are wet, which I hate.

Our waiter appears with a stack of clean napkins. He snaps one open and hands it to Dennis Engelman, then he layers the rest on the spilled water, sopping it up. "There you go, miss," he says, winking at me. "It could happen to anyone. Are you ready to place your order?" he asks the three of us.

"*Yes,*" my mother says, sounding as if she wants to get this dinner disaster over with as soon as possible. "I'll have your manicotti special, please."

"And you, Emma?" Dennis Engelman asks, putting me before him—even though I have been kind of mean to him.

Mom smiles, because she likes good manners.

"I'll have your lobster," I tell the waiter, copying the way my mom said it. "I mean I'll have *two* lobsters," I correct myself, feeling inspired— because lobster is the most expensive food on the menu. *This* will teach Dennis Engelman a lesson about inviting a kid out to dinner when she doesn't want to go.

Real lobsters in the ocean are very interesting, by the way. They shed their shells a bunch of times before they start to look like themselves. But I think live lobsters in supermarket tanks just

Lobsters can grow back missing claws!

look *sad*, all stacked up on top of each other with rubber bands snapped tight around their poor little claws. That's just *wrong*.

People should not eat lobsters unless they catch them themselves with their bare hands, with no rubber bands on the lobsters, so it's a fair fight. That's what I think.

Although tonight, I'm making an expensive exception.

Mom practically snorts, she is so annoyed with me. "Don't be ridiculous, Emma—you've never tasted lobster before in your life," she says, whisking my menu away from me. "She'll have spaghetti and meatballs," she tells our waiter. "The child's portion."

Dennis Engelman looks as though he's about to say something, but then he seems to think twice, and he keeps his mouth shut—which is a smart thing for him to do, under the circumstances.

I guess he knows my mother better than I thought.

X X X

Mom and Dennis Engelman get soup and salad with their dinner and I don't, but I don't even care. The soup has weird-looking beans in it, and at the very top of their salads is that pale hairy lettuce that thinks it's so great, but it's not. It's just bitter and scary.

I snag a fourth pat of butter and load up another breadstick.

After about a hundred hours, the waiter shows up with our dinners: two manicottis, which look like skinny burritos, and one spaghetti and meatballs. "Would you like cheese with that, miss?" the waiter asks me.

"Yes, *please*," I say with actual enthusiasm, because cheese is my second-favorite food group—after chocolate. Anthony and I have that in common, I guess. So the waiter starts grating small golden pieces from a napkin-wrapped hunk of cheese he is holding, which is something I have never seen before. I watch the cheese pile up in a fluffy little mountain on my meatballs. It's getting higher and higher.

And higher.

And *higher.*

"Say when," the waiter murmurs, but I don't say a word. I feel as though I have been hypnotized by that mountain of cheese.

Also, I want to see if he'll cover my entire plate, if I don't tell him not to.

My mom and Dennis Engelman have been gazing into each other's eyes, which Annie Pat would just *love*, but suddenly Mom sees what is going on. "That'll be fine, thanks," she says to the waiter, then she gives me a look.

We pick up our forks. I start poking around in the cheese for my very first meatball. I can't help it, but my mouth is watering like crazy.

And I don't know how it happens, exactly—but the second my fork touches it, one of my meatballs goes flying out from under the cheese and hits my mom right on the chest.

Bo-o-o-i-i-ng!

And it slides down the front of her almost-new, silky-soft, pale-pink dress, leaving a bright orange spaghetti sauce trail behind it.

I cannot even catch my breath, this is so bad.

"Oh," Mom says, stunned, and Dennis Engelman's glasses shine with sympathy.

"It's okay, Maggie," he says softly. "It's okay, Emma."

He's trying to make us *both* feel better!

What a crazy time to start liking him. A little bit, anyway.

"Acqua frizzante," the flustered waiter says, appearing out of nowhere with a bottle of bubble-water and a clean napkin. He soaks the napkin, then leans over me and starts dabbing at my mom. Dennis Engelman looks as though he wants to say something to the guy about touching her, but he can't figure out *what.*

"Let's just leave it," Mom says to the waiter, taking the napkin away. "I'll bring the dress in to the cleaner

in the morning. Everything's fine, just fine." She even manages a smile.

But everything's *not* fine, because like I said before, my mom hasn't bought a new dress in a long, long time. And I ruined it.

"I'm sorry," I whisper, staring down at my blurry plate. "It was an accident."

My mother reaches over and gives me a one-armed hug. "I know it was, sweetie," she tells me. "And it's just a dress. There's no real harm done.

Want me to cut up those noodles for you?" she asks, just to prove there are no hard feelings.

I nod, because I don't know how to twirl yet.

"Well!" Mom says, looking up at Dennis Engelman while she cuts. "I'll bet you haven't ever had *this* much excitement on a dinner date before."

"I was just thinking that myself," Dennis Engelman says, matching her smile.

And he shares one with me, too.

✕ 10 ✕
Do-Over

"Guess what?" Mom asks me the next morning, Saturday, as I am spooning cereal into my sleepy mouth while watching cartoons on TV. I am eating fast so my cereal won't get soggy, which I hate.

"What?" I mumble, trying not to dribble any milk.

"There's a call for you," she says, holding out her shiny and complicated new cell phone, which she bought because she gave up on finding the old one.

Annie Pat Masterson is the most likely person

to call me on a Saturday morning, but how would she know my mom's cell number? I swallow my bite of cereal, press Mute on the TV remote, and take mom's very small new phone in my hand. I don't know the buttons yet, so I hope I don't accidentally cut off whoever it is on the other end.

My cereal is practically falling apart in the bowl, I notice gloomily. "Hello?" I say.

"Hi, Emma," a man's voice—not my dad's—says, sounding cheerful. "It's me, Dennis. Dennis Engelman. Your mom's friend?" he adds, making it a question.

Like I don't remember him! "Hello," I say again. "And thank-you-for-the-very-nice-time-last-night," I add, just in case my mom is eavesdropping. "How may I assist you?" I add politely.

This sounds just right, I think, pleased. It sounds official, but not overly friendly, like I'm some waggy-tailed dog.

Dennis Engelman laughs. "I thought we might

have a do-over, Emma," he says. "That's how you may assist me."

"What does that mean?" I ask, suspicious, because if he thinks I'm going through one more *Ordeal by Meatball* disguised as a fancy dinner, he's got another think coming.

"'Do-over' means that we take another stab at having some fun together, and getting to know each other a little better," he explains.

Okay. Now, in my opinion, I think "taking a stab" at *anything* sounds pretty violent, kind of like how a serial killer might talk. Think about it, Mom.

But she says he's okay.

"You'd get to choose this time, Emma," Dennis Engelman continues, like he's coaxing me. "Some really fun place to have lunch today for you, me, and your mom—and maybe even a friend, if you'd like. My treat. Anywhere at all, Emma. And maybe a movie afterward?"

"Any place for lunch? And *any* movie?" I ask, not really believing it, because *one*, movies are expensive, even in the afternoon, and *two*, it is just about impossible to get a grown-up to take you to something you really want to see.

Which, in this case, is a new movie about a beautiful girl my age who lives near a crystal castle, and she discovers that she is really the princess of all the elves and fairies in the realm. Cynthia Harbison told me all about it last week at school. It's called *Silla's Crystal Kingdom*, and it's in 3-D, and it costs extra for the

glasses—which I think Dennis Engleman will have to wear on top of his other glasses, if we actually go. I guess that will move him down a notch from medium handsome to just sort of handsome, but I don't think my mom will mind.

"So, what do you say?" Dennis Engelman asks patiently.

"I say *sure*," I tell him shyly. "If it's okay with my mom, I mean. And okay with Annie Pat's mom, too, but she'll probably say yes, because they have a new baby over there. So she says yes to everything."

"Good. Where would you like to go for lunch?" he asks. "Maybe I can make a reservation."

"Well, there's this one place," I say, daring to dream. "I haven't actually been there, not personally, but I don't think it's really a reservation kind of place, because it wasn't planned for grown-ups. It's for desserts, mainly, and birthday parties, and it's got silver balloons, and sparkles, and everything. But this girl I know told me they have regular food, too. Oh, and they even have a giant golden birdcage with a table inside," I add, excited, trying to remember all the stuff Cynthia was bragging about. "It's called *Galore!*," I add. "It's pink, and it's across from the Oak Glen post office. But you wouldn't know where that is," I add, remembering suddenly that he lives in some other town.

"I'll look it up," he tells me. "You call your friend, and your mom and I will work out all the details. Bye, Emma. See you later."

"Bye," I say, hoping I can figure out a way to turn off Mom's new phone before Dennis Engelman changes his mind. I press End, and hope that's it, which it is.

Wow, I think, this is kind of like bribery.

But it's *working*.

X X X

It is almost six thirty at night by the time Mom and I unlock the front door and stumble inside. My stomach is full of my chili dog and the hot fudge sundae with a cherry on top—eaten inside that golden cage!—and my brain is full of beautiful crystal castles and billowing white movie clouds and really cute fairies and elves.

Annie Pat liked the movie too, and she *loved* the 3-D glasses.

"My ears," Mom says, plopping her purse onto a living room chair and flinging herself on the sofa. "They're still ringing with all those *songs*. But in a good way," she adds quickly, smiling at me.

"I know," I tell her happily. "Weren't they cute? And wasn't Silla *adorable*, with her silky golden hair falling down to the back of her knees?"

"Adorable," Mom agrees.

"I'm gonna grow out *my* hair," I say, snuggling in next to my mom for a cuddle.

"Down to the back of your knees?" she asks, giving me a squeeze. "We can barely get the brush through it now, honey. Not that I don't love your hair just the way it is."

"Tangled up," I say, sighing.

"Some things just seem to have a way of getting tangled up," my mother replies, and I suddenly get the feeling that she's not talking about hair anymore. She's probably talking in Mom-code about her and my dad, or maybe about Dennis Engelman and me. Or even about divorce.

"Yeah," I agree quietly. "And sometimes you can't use conditioner on the tangles."

"But you can straighten them out just the same," Mom says. "Given time."

"I guess," I say, giving up on the code. "Annie Pat thinks Dennis Engelman is handsome," I tell her after a quiet moment or two. My head is curled against her chest, so I'm not looking at her. It's easier to talk that way.

"Really?" Mom says, sounding happy. "And what about you, Emma? Do you like him?"

"He's okay," I mumble. "He knows how to have fun, in an expensive kind of way. Not that I'm complaining."

"I'm glad you had a good time, darling," my mother says.

"Mom?" I ask after another quiet moment, when the only sound has been the furnace thumping on, and the clock on the mantel chiming seven, because it's always twelve minutes early.

"Mmm?" my mother says, sounding drowsy.

"Does Daddy know about Dennis Engelman?"

She's awake again. I can feel it.

"I may have mentioned him in an e-mail, Emma," she says carefully.

That's a *yes*, by the way.

"Why?" Mom asks. "Does that bother you, Emma?"

"A little," I confess. "Even though I know it doesn't really make any sense, because Daddy got married again, and everything."

"And everything," Mom echoes faintly.

"And Mr. Engelman doesn't even *know* Daddy," I add. "So it's not like he's being a bad friend to him. And Dennis Engelman is nice to kids," I add, trying to think of all his good points. "And he's quiet during movies, which is important, and he's funny, too. Even Annie Pat says so. She liked the way he pretended to cry at the end of the movie, when the chief elf sacrificed his magic powers to save Silla's life."

"Do you ever think you'll be able to just call him 'Dennis,' Emma?" Mom asks in a fake-teasing way, tickling me under my chin a little, which I usually like.

"Who? Mr. Engelman?" I ask, stalling for time while I try to figure out an easy answer to a not-easy question.

"Yes, *Mr. Engelman*," Mom says.

"I guess," I finally say. "It depends on how long he's gonna be around."

"It might be for a while," Mom says, laughing and cuddling me at the same time. "For a long, long time, even."

"Then I'll think about it," I tell her. "It's a definite maybe, Mom."

"I can live with that," Mom says, smoothing my hair away from my face, which is something I also like.

"And I could live with some soup," I murmur, even though half an hour ago, I thought I'd never be hungry again.

"Me too," my mom says. "I'll go heat some up, okay?"

"For just us two," I say, giving her hand one last squeeze.

"Just us two," Mom agrees. "For now, anyway," she calls over her shoulder from down the hall.

"I guess I can live with that," I tell the empty room.

✗ 11 ✗

Explaining things to Anthony Scarpetto

"Was the spaghetti good when you went to that fancy restaurant?" Anthony asks five nights later at his house, because my mom is out with Dennis again—alone, this time.

Spaghetti is Anthony's favorite food, so he is waiting for an answer, even though he has already heard all the now-funny details about the bad things that happened that night. "Yeah," I tell him. "You would have loved it, Ant."

"I'm back to Anthony," Anthony says, sighing. "Because Natalie said she'd squish me if I was an ant. And she could do it, too," he adds, shuddering. Then he snaps his blunt-nosed scissors a couple of times, getting ready to attack the long, narrow strips of construction paper fanned out across his little desk. We are making paper chains for Christmas, which is almost here.

I wonder if Dennis will get me a present?

"What do you want for Christmas, Emma?" Anthony asks me.

"Lots of stuff," I tell him. "But mainly CDs, clothes, and a microscope, so I can look at feathers and things up close."

Not a *nuclear* microscope, of course. But a real, grown-up one would be nice.

"What do you want, Anthony?" I say, because I can tell he really wants me to ask. That's why he brought it up, probably. It's how people are when they talk, even kids.

Anthony puts his *shhh* finger to his lips, shifts his eyes around like he is looking for spies, then runs over to his bed as fast as his chunky little legs can carry him. He is wearing faded Spider-Man underpants and his pajama top, but I have stopped trying to improve his wardrobe.

He pulls a piece of paper out from under his pillow. On it are spelled the words "*E M A*" in green crayon letters and "*F A R T R K*" in red crayon letters.

Uh-oh. This reminds me of my fake word search, only worse.

"Is that supposed to be a bad word?" I ask, pointing to a few of the red letters. "Because you shouldn't—"

"It spells *fire truck*," Anthony says patiently, tracing his finger under the word. "My mom told me to write down what I want for Christmas, and so I did."

"And what does this other word spell?" I ask, pointing to it.

Anthony laughs. "It spells *Emma*, Emma!" he says. "Because I want to get a big sister for Christmas. Only she has to be just like you."

"Aw, thanks, Anthony," I say, because this is a major, major compliment. "Only you can't ever have a *big* sister, because that means she'd be older than you. And you're always going to be the oldest kid in your family."

"I'm the *only* kid in my

family," Anthony points out. "And I can have a big sister if I want one. *The End*," he adds, scowling. He snaps his scissors at me a couple of times to emphasize his point.

For some goofy reason I can't let this big sister thing pass. "You can maybe have a *little* sister one day," I try to explain, "or a little brother. But you'll always be the oldest kid in your family. It's just the way things are, Anthony."

"But I don't *want* a little brother," Anthony shouts, and *ka-pow!*—construction paper strips go flying everywhere.

I can see that I was an optimist to think we would get enough paper chains done tonight to decorate both our Christmas trees.

"Don't cry, Anthony," I say, trying to calm him down.

"I wanna be the only boy in our family," Anthony wails. "And anyway, Mommy's not even preg-mump."

"Pregnant. Pregnant," I say, nervously looking around as I correct him. Because what is Anthony's mom going to think if she walks into the room right now and I'm talking about how babies are born?

Especially when I'm not even sure of all the details myself?

Explaining things to Anthony Scarpetto is tough, but someone has to try. "Look, Anthony," I say. "First your mom and your dad had you, so you're the oldest kid. And if they have another kid, it'll be—"

Anthony springs to his feet in a rage. "You're not the boss of me," he cries. "And I can have a big sister if I want one, because *I've been good*. Anyway, it's not up to you, it's up to Santa! *The End*."

"Well, you're not being very good right now," I grumble, picking up the construction paper strips.

"What?"

"I said, *Okay!* What-*ever*," I tell him, and he settles right down.

"What-*ever*," he echoes, satisfied. "What-*ever*."

"But don't go around saying that," I tell him, nervous once more. "Because it's kind of rude, according to my mom."

"Okay," Anthony says, searching for his scissors. "So do you like him now?" he asks me after he has found the scissors and is looking around for something to cut.

"Who?"

"The falling-napkin guy who took you out for flying meatballs," Anthony says. "Do you like him?"

I flap my own construction paper strips back and forth like a skinny fan and frown while I think about Anthony's question. "Dennis is okay," I finally say. "He really is. Of course, I wish my mom would just stay home with *me*. But if she has to go out with someone, I guess he's not the worst person in the world."

"But—what if he wants to be your new dad-dy?" Anthony asks, worried.

"Well, he can't be my daddy," I snap. "Because I already have a real one. In London. *So The End* to you, too."

"I never seen your real daddy," Anthony says, his brown eyes narrowing with suspicion.

"'I never *saw* him,'" I say, correcting him.

"So, ha ha," Anthony says, like he's just won an argument.

I just sigh, because I have walked right into that crazy, invisible Anthony wall once more. It's hard to avoid it, really.

"But Merry Christmas early, Emma," Anthony says. "Even though you're so wrong about stuff. And I *am* going to get a fire truck, because I already seen it in the hall closet."

"Congratulations," I tell him. "And Merry Christmas early to you, too, by the way."

"What-*ever*," Anthony says, busy with a few construction paper strips once more.

But then he flashes me a sideways grin, and all of a sudden I feel sure that everything is going to be okay.

I'm pretty sure, anyway!

turn the page to peek inside more books
featuring the irrepressible Emma . . .

x x x

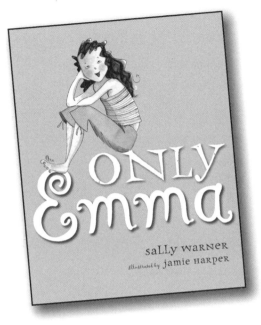

ONLY Emma

saLLy waRNeR

illustrated by jamie haRPeR

You are always the boss—
of other kids, anyway—when
you are at your own house.
That's the rule, even though
no one ever wrote it down.

Until now.

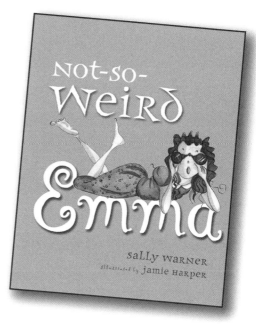

NoT-So-Weird Emma

saLLy waRNeR
illustrated by jamie haRpeR

"Oh, let's not get carried away, Cynthia," I say, which is actually something my mom says to me fairly often. Only she calls me *Emma*, not *Cynthia*, of course.

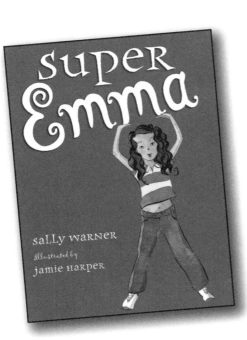

Mom says "in a pickle" when she means that a person is in trouble. Or else she says "in a jam." She likes food talk, I guess.

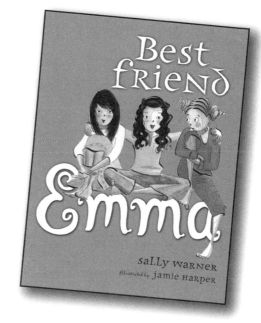

Annie Pat and I are getting ready for Thanksgiving—ten days away, Mom says—by stretching our stomachs. You have to do this from the inside, with food, because outside stretching doesn't work. We already tried that.

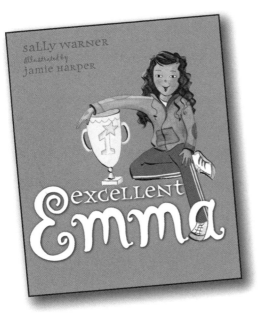

I take a deep breath. "I want this gold star to be yours, in honor of us being such excellent friends." And I give her one of my stars—a little slowly, but I do it.

And it's my best star, too.